For Tom
D.B.
For my little bears, Willow and Iolo,
because I love you xx
R.H.

First published in 2013 by Nosy Crow Ltd
The Crow's Nest, 10a Lant Street
London SE1 1QR
www.nosycrow.com

ISBN 978 0 85763 236 4 (HB)
ISBN 978 0 85763 242 5 (PB)

Nosy Crow and associated logos are trademark
and/or registered trademarks of Nosy Crow Ltd.

Text copyright © David Bedford 2013
Illustrations copyright © Rebecca Harry 2013

The right of David Bedford to be identified as the author and
of Rebecca Harry to be identified as the illustrator of this work has been asserted.

A CIP catalogue record for this book is available from the British Library.

Printed in China

10 9 8 7 6 5 4 3 2 1

Because I Love You

David Bedford • Rebecca Harry

At the end of a beautiful, golden day,
it was time for Little Bear to go to bed.
But as Little Bear's mummy bent down to give
him a goodnight kiss, Little Bear looked
up sadly, and said,

"Mummy,
I don't think I've had
any love today."

Little Bear's mummy smiled
and hugged her little bear.
"Not enough love?" she said.
"Why, I'm sure I've given
you lots of love today."

"But I don't remember any love,"
said Little Bear.

"Well," said Mummy Bear,
"then let's remember together . . ."

"Do you remember our walk to the meadow early this morning?
Didn't we have fun kicking up the fallen leaves?"

"And then we rested in the warm grass,"
said Mummy Bear,
"and watched the clouds race by."

"And I thought one cloud looked
like me!" said Little Bear.

"Yes," smiled Mummy Bear,
"but I said no other little bear could
look as sweet as my little bear."

"Because you love me?"
asked Little Bear.

"Because I love you,"
smiled Mummy Bear.

"Then the clouds turned
grey and dark,"
said Mummy Bear.
"Do you remember?"

"Yes, and it rained and rained!"
cried Little Bear.

"We got **very** wet," said Mummy Bear,
"but I let you splash in **all** the puddles
because you **love** to splash."

"And when the rain turned into a blustery storm and you were a little bit scared, I found you shelter," said Mummy Bear. "You know I'll **always** protect you from things that scare you."

"Because you love me?" asked Little Bear.

"Because I love you," smiled Mummy Bear.

"I don't like storms," said Little Bear.

"I know," said Mummy Bear, "and that's why
we snuggled up and watched and waited until
the sun came out again.
Do you remember what we saw then,
my little bear?"

"A rainbow!" laughed Little Bear,
"and I wanted to touch it!"

"So I lifted you as high as you could go,
to try and reach the rainbow," said Mummy Bear.
"I'll always help you – whatever you reach for."

"Because you love me?"
asked Little Bear.

"Because I love you,"
smiled Mummy Bear.

"And now I remember
what we did next,"
said Little Bear.
"We found nuts and berries
for our supper!"

"We even found your favourites," said Mummy Bear,
"lovely, sweet blueberries, remember?"

"And you put sticky honey on top,"
said Little Bear, licking his lips.

"Yes, that's right!" said Mummy Bear.

"And then I sang your favourite song as we washed your sticky paws," laughed Mummy Bear. "I always know your favourite things."

"Because you love me?"
asked Little Bear.

"Because I love you,"
smiled Mummy Bear.

Then Little Bear yawned and said,
"Mummy, I want to give you
a big, big hug."

"Because you love me?"
smiled Mummy Bear.

"Because I love you,"
said Little Bear.

"We have had lots of love today,"
said Little Bear sleepily.

"We have lots of love every day,"
Mummy Bear whispered.

Then, curled up tight
in his mummy's arms,
Little Bear smiled and slept,
with enough love inside
him to last the
whole night through.

Because I Love You